GRANDPA'S TRACTOR

MICHAEL GARLAND

BOYDS MILLS PRESS
Honesdale, Pennsylvania

Boyds Mills Press, Inc.
815 Church Street
Honesdale, Pennsylvania 18431
Printed in the United States of America

ISBN: 978-1-59078-762-5

Library of Congress Control Number: 2010929544

First edition
The text of this book is set in 16-point Minion Pro.
The illustrations are done digitally.

10 9 8 7 6 5 4 3 2 1

For all the family farmers and their tractors

Grandpa Joe and Timmy were going to see the old farm where Grandpa Joe used to live when he was a boy.

Grandpa Joe told Timmy that the farm had been sold long ago,
but there was still something there to see.

When they arrived, the first thing they saw was an old boarded-up
farmhouse and a faded red barn with the roof fallen in.

"It's hard to believe," Grandpa said, "but this was a beautiful place.
There were no other houses around here, just open fields and pastures for the cows."

Grandpa Joe and Timmy walked through the weeds past the barn.

"There it is!" said Grandpa.

"What's that?" asked Timmy as he pointed to a rusty hulk of machinery.

"That's the most important thing a farmer can own. It's a tractor," Grandpa said with a sad smile.

Timmy stared at the old tractor. It was covered with rust.
Only a few bits of red paint were left. The tires were flat, and saplings
were growing out of the engine.

"When I was a boy, that tractor was new, with shiny red paint.
My father used it for almost all the chores around the farm,"
Grandpa said proudly.

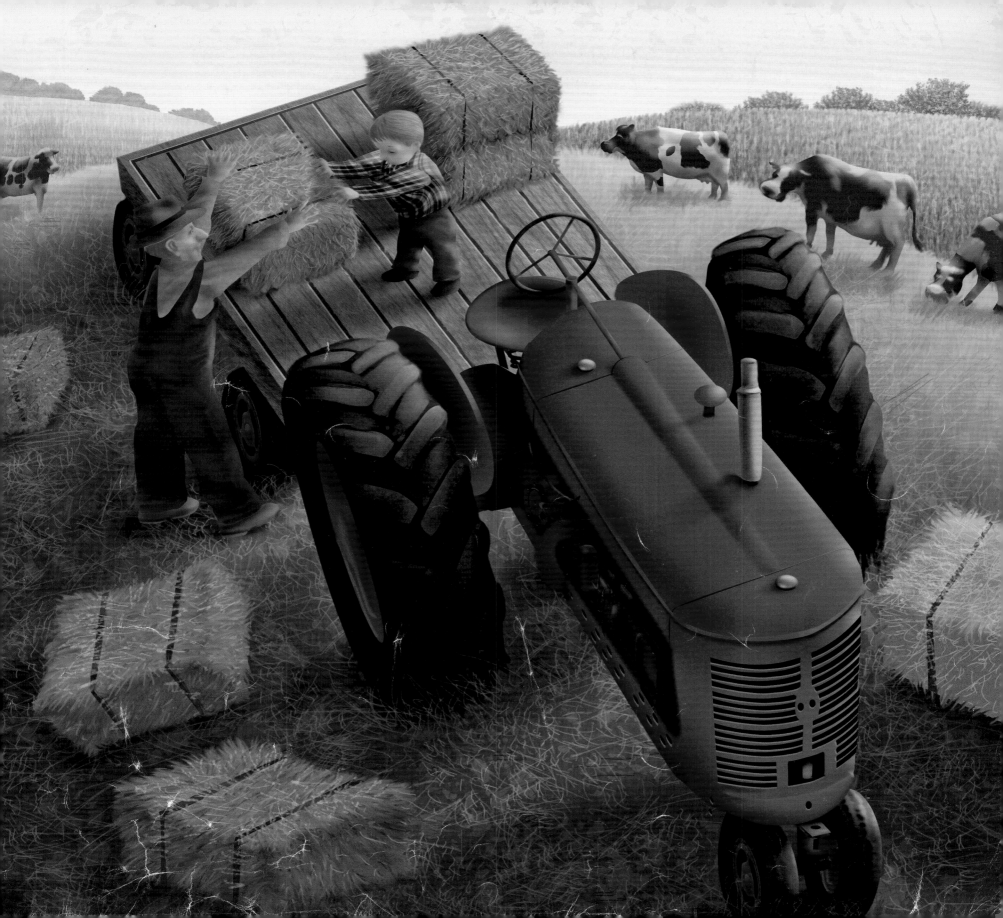

"When I was your age, my dad let me sit on his lap and steer the tractor as we plowed the fields," Grandpa said with a happier smile.

The more Grandpa Joe talked about the tractor, the more excited he became. "After we plowed, we would plant the seeds for corn or alfalfa to feed the cows."

Timmy imagined the tractor when it was shiny and red, with its motor rumbling and with tires that were new and round.

"When it was harvest time, we gathered the corn and hay and stored all of it in the silo for the cows to eat during the winter." Grandpa pointed to the tumbled-down tower that used to be the silo.

"In the fall, my father would hitch a wagon onto the back and ride the whole family up to the orchard to pick apples." Grandpa laughed. "I would eat almost as many as I picked!"

By now, Timmy could see the shiny red tractor even though he was standing right next to a pile of rust.

"We would load the wagon with our corn and squash and pumpkins and sell them down by the road."

Timmy remembered his own mom and dad buying a pumpkin last year for Halloween.

"My father could fix this tractor no matter what broke. He knew every nut and bolt. He could take it all apart and put it right back together. I used to help him."

Timmy wished he could fix the broken-down tractor right now.

"In the winter, we would hook a sled to the tractor and haul firewood to heat the house," Grandpa said.

Timmy tried to imagine winter even though it was summer.

"At Christmastime, Mother would bundle up all the children and Dad would give us a ride on the sled back into the woods so we could pick out our Christmas tree."

When Timmy looked at the old farmhouse, he could picture the smoke rising from the chimney and the lights from the Christmas tree twinkling through the window.

"Grandpa, thanks for bringing me here," Timmy said.
"I never knew tractors were so important."

About *Grandpa's Tractor*

When someone says "red tractor," he or she is probably talking about the Farmall red tractor. That never occurred to me until I started thinking about the rusty old tractor embedded in a hillside close to my home. The tractor slept in the weeds, behind an old farmhouse and rickety barn. I had passed it for years without giving it a second thought. Then slowly I started to imagine a farmer getting off that tractor fifty years ago and never getting back on. That was the beginning of *Grandpa's Tractor*.

I decided to knock on the door of the farmhouse. As I waited, I studied the house's peeling paint and leaking gutters. When the door opened, I met the very same farmer who had climbed down from the tractor fifty years ago. He told me how he sold off his farmland so houses could be built. The farmer also told me how the tractor was used to do many of the hard jobs around the farm. It plowed the earth and planted the crops. It harvested the corn and hay and vegetables that fed people and animals. The retired farmer said he was clearing brush the day the tractor broke down, all those years ago.

That's when I began to learn about Farmall tractors. A company named International Harvester made Farmall tractors from 1923 until 1975 in Rock Island, Illinois.

All the farms near my home have one or two. Some tractors are seventy years old and still working every day! No wonder farmers love them so much.

—M.G.